The Dangers of Drug Abuse

YOU ARE NOT ALONE

OPIOIDS AND OPIATES:
THE SILENT EPIDEMIC

Chronic Pain and Prescription Painkillers
The Dangers of Drug Abuse
The Heroin Crisis
Preventing and Treating Addiction
Who Is Using Opioids and Opiates?

OPIOIDS AND OPIATES:
THE SILENT EPIDEMIC

The Dangers
of Drug Abuse

JODEE REDMOND

MASON CREST
PHILADELPHIA

Mason Crest
450 Parkway Drive, Suite D
Broomall, PA 19008
www.masoncrest.com

©2018 by Mason Crest, an imprint of National Highlights, Inc.

Printed and bound in the United States of America.

CPSIA Compliance Information: Batch #OPO2017.
For further information, contact Mason Crest at 1-866-MCP-Book.

First printing
1 3 5 7 9 8 6 4 2

Library of Congress Cataloging-in-Publication Data

on file at the Library of Congress
ISBN: 978-1-4222-3824-0 (hc)
ISBN: 978-1-4222-7964-9 (ebook)

Opioids and Opiates: The Silent Epidemic series ISBN: 978-1-4222-3822-6

QR CODES AND LINKS TO THIRD-PARTY CONTENT

Table of Contents

1: Drug Abuse and Addiction 7
2: Opioids and their Physical Effects 15
3: Drug Abuse and Mental Health 29
4: The Ways a Drug Conviction Affect Your Life......37
5: The Effects of Opioids on Families 49

Series Glossary of Key Terms..................................58
Further Reading 59
Internet Resources 60
Index 62
Photo Credits/About the Author............................64

KEY ICONS TO LOOK FOR:

Words to understand: These words with their easy-to-understand definitions will increase the reader's understanding of the text while building vocabulary skills.

Sidebars: This boxed material within the main text allows readers to build knowledge, gain insights, explore possibilities, and broaden their perspectives by weaving together additional information to provide realistic and holistic perspectives.

Educational Videos: Readers can view videos by scanning our QR codes, providing them with additional educational content to supplement the text. Examples include news coverage, moments in history, speeches, iconic sports moments and much more!

Text-dependent questions: These questions send the reader back to the text for more careful attention to the evidence presented there.

Research projects: Readers are pointed toward areas of further inquiry connected to each chapter. Suggestions are provided for projects that encourage deeper research and analysis.

Series glossary of key terms: This back-of-the book glossary contains terminology used throughout this series. Words found here increase the reader's ability to read and comprehend higher-level books and articles in this field.

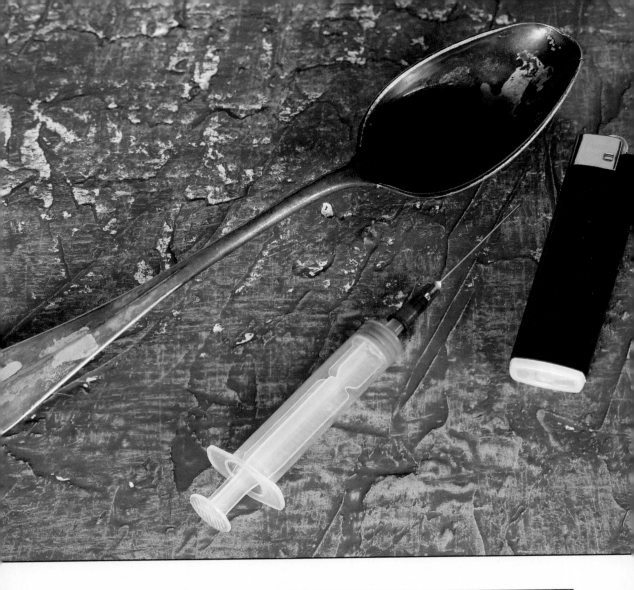

 ## Words to Understand in This Chapter

chronic—a problem or issue that lasts for a long time or constantly recurs.

neurotransmitters—chemicals that are released at the end of a nerve and carry messages to other parts of the body.

stereotypes—an oversimplified idea of a certain type of person, group, or thing that is widely held.

1

◄ *Opioids are a class of drugs that include the illegal drug heroin, as well as a variety of prescription pain relievers such as oxycodone, hydrocodone, codeine, morphine, and fentanyl.*

Drug Abuse and Addiction

Drug abuse is a common problem in modern society. At one time, it was thought to signal a lack of judgment or a personal failure on the part of the addicted person. Many people thought that drug abuse and addiction was a problem that was limited only to certain types of people or those who lived in specific neighborhoods. Such *stereotypes* still exist today.

However, drug addiction and abuse is a problem that affects people from every race, culture, religion and socioeconomic level. Drug abuse can affect people from any background.

What is Drug Addiction?

Research shows that addiction is complicated. It is now thought that addiction is a brain disorder, not a lack of

Did You Know?

Dopamine neurons make up less than one percent of the brain. These are called the "pleasure chemical." All mammals have them, as well as turtles and other more "simple" animals! Taking drugs like opiates produces a higher level of reward in the brain than natural rewards, such as eating a meal or participating in a fun activity.

willpower or something that happens only to people who are "weak." Addiction is a *chronic* disease, and the urge to abuse drugs is a symptom. This urge persists even though the drug addict faces negative consequences to their drug use. These negative consequences may include health problems, difficulties at school or at work, and legal problems like getting arrested or being imprisoned.

Most people who become addicted to drugs believe that they can stop using whenever they want to, at least when they start using. They may not know about the dangers of drug abuse. They may think that they are stronger or smarter than the drugs they are taking and will be able to do something to rise above their effects. Since drug addiction is a brain disease, this is rarely the case. Most people who become addicted to drugs need professional help to stop.

How Addiction Develops Over Time

Each drug produces a specific type of effect when a person takes it, including alcohol. Some of them make the person feel more energetic, while others produce a feeling of deep relaxation. A person's brain cells respond to the drugs their body is taking. (The brain also responds to the hormones and chemicals that the body produces naturally.) Over time, and with repeated exposure, the drugs interfere with the way the brain works.

The *neurotransmitters* move through the brain. These special chemicals are made to have a particular effect on the brain once they reach specific cell surfaces called receptor proteins. Each one of the receptor proteins is formed in a way so that it recognizes a specific neurotransmitter. The two of them fit together, much in the same way that a charger for a digital

 ## What Are Opioids

Opiates are the name for a variety of drugs derived from the opium poppy. Examples of opiates include opium, morphine, heroin, and codeine. They can be used to relieve moderate-to-severe pain.

Natural opiates have been used as pain relievers for thousands of years. Hippocrates, who is called "the father of medicine," was familiar with the pain-relieving properties of the opium poppy. He wrote about drinking a combination of white poppy juice and nettle seeds to treat a number of conditions, including internal discomforts and concerns of women. Opiates were appreciated for their sedative qualities, too. Ancient Greeks, Romans, and Arabs used them for this purpose.

Opioids are medicines that have a similar painkilling effect as opiates, but they are created in laboratories. These drugs are sold under brand names such as Vicodin, OxyContin, or Dilaudid.

device fits into its port. If you don't have the right size of plug, it simply won't fit. The same thing is true for neurotransmitters and receptor proteins. They need to be the right "match" or they won't be able to recognize each other and take the next step. In the case of a cell phone, that would be to recharge the battery. For a neurotransmitter, the next step is for it to travel to another cell.

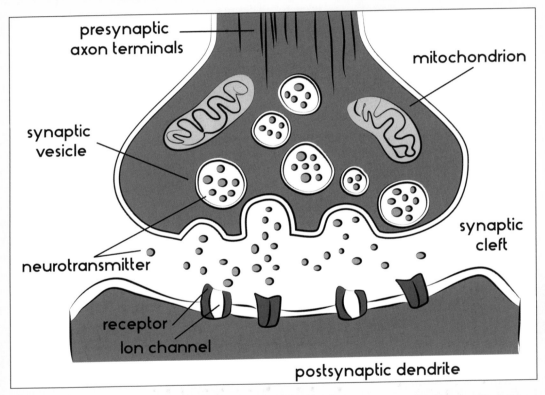

Drugs alter the way people think, feel, and behave by disrupting communication between nerve cells (neurons) in the brain. Neurons are separated by small spaces called synapses. Messages are passed from cell to cell across the synapse by specialized molecules, called neurotransmitters, which bind to receptors on the nerve cells. Prescription opioids and heroin produce effects that are similar to—but stronger than—those produced by the neurotransmitters endorphin and enkephalin: reduced pain, decreased alertness, and slowed respiration.

Educational Video

For a short video on common misconceptions about drug abuse and addiction, scan here:

In a situation where a cell gets exposed to a level of neurotransmitter that is too high, the cell takes action. It mops up any excess chemical and stores it for use later on. This process is called "reuptake." It stops too many chemicals from being active at once.

When a person uses addictive drugs, it can interfere with the natural chemical balance in the brain. Some of them block the reuptake process, and others interfere with the brain's ability to release neurotransmitters in the first place. There are a number of neurotransmitters in the brain. Several of them have been associated with addiction. Some of their names are dopamine, serotonin, substance P, and gamma-aminobutyric acid (GABA).

The first link between brain chemistry and opiates was found in 1973. Dr. Solomon Snyder of Johns Hopkins University and Candace Pert, who was his graduate student at the time, discovered that the brain has opium receptors. Pert had been using radioactive morphine in an attempt to find the receptor and prove the theory, but had been unsuccessful. Once she changed her strategy and decided to use naloxone, a different compound, she found that opiates bind to the brain's receptors.

When someone starts taking drugs like opioids, they stimulate the brain's chemical pleasure centers. These are called endorphins, and the body naturally produces them during exercise, when people laugh, listen to music, eat chocolate or do other enjoyable activities. Drug takers get an artificial high from the drugs they take. Over time and as a person continues to use drugs, the opiate receptors in their brain stay full. At that point, the addict's brain has turned off some of its receptors. The person needs to take more of the drug in order to

According to the American Society of Addiction Medicine, an estimated 21,000 adolescents (age 12 to 17) used heroin in 2015. Approximately 5,000 were current heroin users.

achieve the same effect. It becomes desensitized to the presence of the drug. As a result, the addict needs to take larger doses to get the same effect.

Whether someone takes drugs derived from opium poppies or those made in a laboratory, the brain responds to them in the same manner on a purely chemical level.

A person may make a choice to take drugs in the first place. Once the addiction becomes established, they no longer have a choice about whether they will continue to use drugs. The addict's brain chemistry has changed as a result of their drug use.

 ## Text-Dependent Questions

1. What are some of the stereotypes about people who abuse drugs or become addicts?
2. Can you name the researchers who found the link between opiates and brain chemistry?
3. Name some activities that cause the brain to produce endorphins ("feel-good" chemicals).

 ## Research Project

Look up the "Just Say No" anti-drug campaign from the 1980s online or in magazines. Find similar anti-drug policies and programs. Do you think these are an effective way to stop young people from using drugs? Write a brief essay about your opinion.

 Words to Understand in This Chapter

chronic pain—pain that lasts for more than three months.

drug dependence—a state that develops from repeated drug use, and which
   results in withdrawal symptoms if the drug use ends.

nephropathy—kidney disease or damage to the kidneys.

palliative care—medical care for a serious or life-threatening illness.

semisynthetic—a natural material or compound that has been chemically
   altered in a laboratory.

vascular dementia—a brain condition that leads to a number of symptoms,
   including memory loss, difficulty with thinking speed, language and con-
   trolling emotions.

withdrawal—a syndrome of often painful physical and psychological symptoms that occurs when an addicted person stops taking a drug.

2

Opioids and their Physical Effects

he United States and Canada are in the midst of an opioid crisis. Drugs like fentanyl and heroin are responsible for multiple overdose deaths on a daily basis in major cities. Dr. David Juurlink, the head of clinical pharmacology and toxicology at Toronto's Sunnybrook Health Sciences Center, remarked in an interview to CBC News that, "There has never been a more dangerous time to source drugs on the street."

For many years, opioid pain medications were usually prescribed only for very specific cases, such as for *palliative care*. Around the late 1990s, doctors began to prescribe these powerful drugs for *chronic pain*.

By around 2006, after a great many prescriptions for OxyContin and other opioid painkillers had been written, medical professionals began to become more aware of the very real problem of opioid addiction. Some doctors stopped prescribing opioid painkillers to their patients. However, this didn't solve the problem, as people who were addicted turned to street drugs—such as heroin or fentanyl—when they could no longer get a supply of drugs from their doctor legally.

Opiates and Opioids

The list of opioid drugs includes a variety of substances. Some of them, called opiates, are derived from the juice of the opium poppy. These include morphine, codeine, heroin, thebaine, and orpivaine. Others are synthetic, meaning they are produced using chemicals in a laboratory. These opioids include demerol, fentanyl, dilaudid, norco, lortab, atarax, methadone, and buprenorphine. Some synthetic opioids are used to treat opioid addiction, such as naloxone and naltrexone.

Other opioid drugs are classified as *semisynthetic*, because they are produced from natural substances that have been modified in a laboratory. These include oxymorphone and oxy-

 ## Educational Video

Scan here to see how opioid drugs interact with receptors in the brain and nervous system:

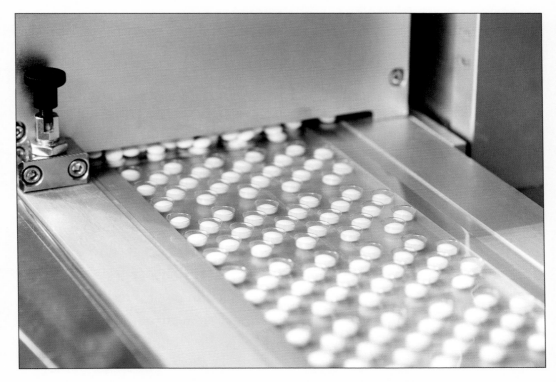

Prescription opioids usually come in pill form and are given to treat severe pain—for example, pain from dental surgery, serious sports injuries, or cancer.

codone, which are synthesized from thebaine; hydrocodine, which is synthesized from codeine; and hydromorphone, which is synthesized from morphine.

Important Opioid Drugs

A substance that is extracted from an opium poppy, **opium** is the source for many narcotics, including morphine and heroin. It is derived from the opium poppy, which is mainly grown in Southeast Asia, Central Asia (in particular, Afghanistan), Mexico, and Colombia. **Morphine** is a highly effective painkiller that is derived from the poppy. Most of the morphine used in the United States is processed into **codeine** and other derivatives. All of these drugs can be taken in orally, smoked, or injected into the bloodstream.

Heroin is one of the most highly addictive and dangerous drugs in the opioid family. Heroin is not available legally in the United States. It is often sold by drug gangs that are connected with drug cartels in Mexico and Latin America. Heroin can be injected, snorted, or smoked.

There are two types of heroin commonly found in the United States. "Black tar" heroin is found primarily in the western states, and generally originated in Mexico. It looks like a black sticky paste. White heroin is found primarily on the East Coast of the United States, and comes from Colombia or from Asia. It is usually sold as a white or brown powder. In either case, the substance that a drug addict buys is often not pure heroin. Drug dealers often mix (or "cut") their product with other drugs to make it more potent, or with other powdery substances to increase the quantity.

During World War II, scientists synthesized **methadone** to combat a shortage of morphine. This drug comes in tablets, discs, oral liquid, or an injectable solution. Methadone is often

 Did You Know?

Withdrawal symptoms from opiates usually start within twelve hours of the last dose of the drug.

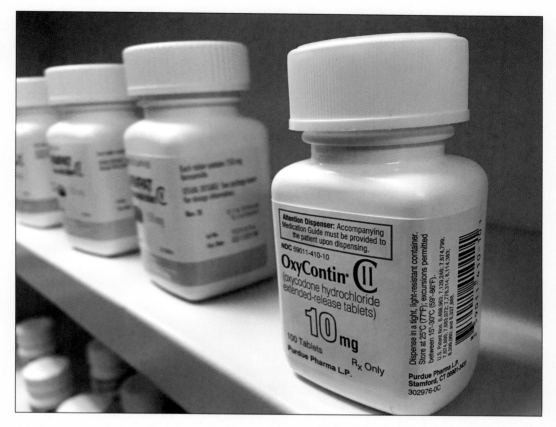

OxyContin was introduced to the public in 1996. Since then, more than $31 billion worth of the pills have been sold, making it the best-selling painkiller in the United States.

provided by drug detoxification facilities in order to treat addiction to heroin or other opioids.

Like methodone, **oxycodone** is a synthesized opioid. Under the brand name OxyContin, it is widely abused. It comes in tablets with multiple dosages. Products such as aspirin and acetaminophen are sometimes combined with it. It can also be taken via injection. Tablets are sometimes crushed and sniffed or dissolved in water and injected. Another method of use is to heat a tablet on a piece of aluminum foil and then inhale the smoke from it.

Hydromorphone is a painkiller that is considerably more powerful than morphine, although its effects do not last as long. It is a legal drug in the United States, and like oxycodone is often prescribed for chronic pain. The usual form of administration is by tablets. However, injection is also possible by crushing the tablets and dissolving them in a solution.

Today, one of the most dangerous opioid painkillers is **Fentanyl**. In 2015, Fentanyl was legally prescribed more than six million times for pain reduction. It is 50 times more powerful than morphine, and dealers of illegal drugs sometimes add Fentanyl to cut heroin to make it more potent. This can have deadly consequences, as a tiny amount of Fentanyl can result in a fatal drug overdose.

How Opioids Work

When an opioid drug enters the body, it binds to certain receptors in the brain. The human body has mu-opioid receptors (MORs) that are receptive to the presence of the drug. The receptors are present in the brain and the body for different reasons:

1. They regulate pain;
2. They are responsible for releasing hormones; and
3. They also stimulate feelings of well-being.

When the body's MORs, which are located in the reward center of the brain, are activated, they cause the neurotrans-

Opioid Addiction Facts

The following statistics were provided by the American Society of Addiction Medicine:

- Most young people who misuse prescription medications are given the drugs for free by either a friend or a relative. People often start sharing unused pain medications, and they are unaware of the dangers.
- Today, approximately 20.5 million people in the United States are living with a substance-abuse problem. Of these, two million people have a problem with prescription drugs and approximately 600,000 have a problem with heroin.
- Close to one-quarter (23 percent) of all people who use heroin become addicted.
- Approximately 52,000 people lost their lives to accidental drug overdoses in 2015, making it the leading cause of accidental death in the United States.
- Eighty percent of new heroin users started out abusing prescription medications.

mitter dopamine to be released. When dopamine is released, it creates a feeling of pleasure. During this phase, the user will feel a "rush" or "high." The intensity of the experience depends upon how much of the drug was ingested, as well as how quickly the drug enters the brain and is able to bind to the opioid receptors.

Over time, an opioid user will need to take larger amounts

of the drug in order to achieve the same effect. At that point, they have developed a tolerance for the drug, because they are no longer able to achieve the results they seek with lower doses. This is true of people to use opioids for pain management, as well as those who take them recreationally, seeking to get high.

Physical Dependence

A person who uses opioids regularly can develop a physical *dependence* on the drugs. This means that the person's body becomes so used to the drug's effects that it cannot function properly without the opioid drug. The person often also develops a psychological dependence, craving the drugs and believing that he or she cannot live without taking them.

If an addicted person tries to stop taking drugs, he or she will experience a variety of unpleasant physical and psychological symptoms, known collectively as withdrawal.

In the early stages of withdrawal, a person may experience agitation or anxiety, difficulty sleeping, muscle aches, cold symptoms, sweating, and exhaustion. As the withdrawal period continues, the symptoms become more intense, and can

 Did You Know?

Muscle spasms from opium withdrawal result in involuntary kicking movements. This is where the term "kicking the habit" came from.

A study by the Centers for Disease Control (CDC) found that women are more likely to have chronic pain, be prescribed prescription pain relievers, be given higher doses, and use them for longer time periods than men. In addition, the study found that women may become dependent on prescription pain relievers more quickly than men.

include painful abdominal cramps, diarrhea, nausea and vomiting, and even hallucinations.

The withdrawal period can last for up to 14 days, depending on the type of opioid, the amount that the person was taking, and the length of time the person had been taking it.

Some people report experiencing psychological symptoms of withdrawal even after the physical symptoms subside. These include feelings of depression, as well as powerful cravings for their drug of choice that last for several months after the last time they used.

How Opioid Drugs Permanently Change the Body

Aging is a normal part of life. Every person has a certain age in years, which is their chronological age. The cells in the body have a biological age, which is determined by a number of factors, such as the person's family history and environment. Certain diseases or behaviors can have an impact on how quickly the cells in a person's body age.

Researchers have found that drug addiction leads to the early onset of age-related diseases. In the same way that smoking leads to cancer and reduces life expectancy among smokers, drug abuse has a negative effect among users. Research is showing that substance abuse and addiction is responsible for accelerated aging of the body's cells. It also leads to a number of other diseases linked to premature death.

Addiction is a chronic disease that affects the brain. When someone is involved in addictive behavior, they are not living a healthy lifestyle. While they may think they have their drug use under control, in fact, their life starts to become a circle that turns into getting high, craving drugs, and then binging. More and more of their energy is taken up to support their addiction,

 Did You Know?

As you age, it's normal for your brain weight to decrease by five percent every 10 years after the age of 40. Some drugs, such as cocaine, will speed up this process to up to twice the normal rate.

Drug abuse can accelerate the aging process.

and there is less room for healthy lifestyle choices, like eating properly, exercising, and getting enough rest.

People who are addicted to opioids are less likely to see a doctor or dentist regularly for checkups. If they do, they aren't likely to admit that they have a drug problem. They may be concerned that the doctor won't want to treat them for their other health issues, so they avoid seeking medical care.

Research has shown that opioid use is linked to a slowdown of cell growth in the body. It also speeds up the rate of cell death. When opioids are used in combination with other drugs,

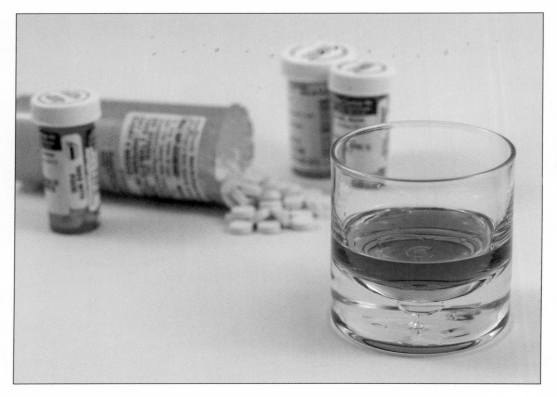

Combining opioids and alcohol can result in permanent heart or liver damage.

the process speeds up even more, such as when cocaine and opioids are used together.

Opioid use, particularly heroin, has also been linked to heart disease and chronic brain small vessel disease. Small vessel disease can lead to *vascular dementia*. According to a 2017 study by Dr. Nelly Alia-Klein, published in the journal *Current Opinion on Behavioral Science*, opiate addiction can lead to a "hyperactive immune-mediated inflammatory state" in the brain. This condition makes a person more likely to develop heart disease. It can also lead to a condition called endocarditis, an infection of the inner lining of the heart. Endocarditis is a potentially life-threatening condition.

When used in combination with alcohol, heroin is known to trigger a serious condition called cirrhosis of the liver, as well as *nephropathy*. This type of kidney disease is linked to diabetes, which means that there is a link to opioid use/addiction and diabetes, as well.

Even though they may not realize it, every time someone with an opioid substance abuse issue uses these types of drugs, they are they are causing the cells in their body to age, and die, at a faster-than-normal rate. This speeds up their body's normal aging process. As a result, they are putting themselves at higher-than-normal risk for age-related diseases and conditions.

 Text-Dependent Questions

1. Which plant is used to manufacture heroin?
2. What powerful opioid is sometimes added to heroin to make it more potent?
3. Name some of the ways that opioid use can affect normal cell aging.

 Research Project

Do you think you would be able to tell if someone you know had a substance abuse problem or do you think they would be able to hide it? Discuss your thoughts.

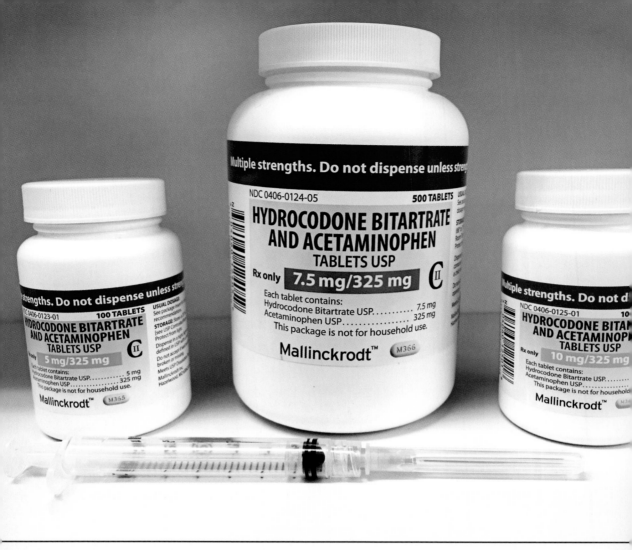

 Words to Understand in This Chapter

dual diagnosis—when a person has an addiction to drugs and/or alcohol and is also living with a mental illness.

self-medication—using drugs or alcohol to treat symptoms of mental illness on one's own, as opposed to seeking professional help.

3

◀ *Some people inaccurately refer to all drugs as narcotics. Only natural, synthetic, or semisynthetic opioids can be properly classified as narcotic drugs. Pictured here is hydrocodone, a semisynthetic opioid pain medication.*

Drug Abuse and Mental Health

Drug abuse and mental health issues are closely related. Often, people who live with a mental illness also have substance abuse issues. This type of *dual diagnosis* is very common.

An addiction to drugs or alcohol doesn't develop in some type of vacuum. Often, it starts because a person is experiencing some type of mental or emotional pain. There are a number of positive ways that someone could choose to deal with stress, anxiety, self-esteem issues or a past traumatic event. They may not have resources or support available to them to get help when they need it. A person may decide to solve the problem themselves because they feel guilty or ashamed to share that something is bothering them.

In the case of a person with a dual diagnosis, it can be difficult to determine which condition came first.

Substance Abuse and Mental Illness: Which Comes First?

Some people who have symptoms of a mental illness don't realize what is happening to them or are reluctant to seek treatment for their condition. Instead, they use drugs or alcohol to treat their symptoms themselves. This type of *self-medication* is quite common.

In the case of opioids, someone may be drawn to these types of drugs for either the initial high that they give to users or the deep sense of relaxation and sleepiness that follows. Drugs in this class would be attractive to people who are looking to feel a burst of pleasure and those who are already feeling anxious or having trouble sleeping and are looking for something to make them feel calmer.

This would be an example where the substance abuse would come first. In other situations, long-term drug abuse can lead to a person developing a mental health problem. In the case of opioids, there is a link between depression and the long-term use of drugs in this class.

What is Depression?

Depression is a very common and potentially serious form of mental illness. Known as a mood disorder, it affects the way a person feels about themselves. It also impacts a person's thoughts and the way they behave. Depression also responds very well to treatment.

The rate of depression tends to increase during the winter holiday season, particularly in November and December, and is often higher during the winter months. However, suicide rates tend to peak in late summer.

It is not the same as grief or feeling sad. These are normal responses to life events. Depression is something deeper, and it robs the affected person of being able to enjoy activities that used to bring pleasure. In order to be diagnosed with depression, the feelings of hopelessness or worthlessness must last continuously for at least two weeks.

Other signs of depression include difficulty sleeping or sleeping too much, lack of appetite or overeating, difficulty concentrating and low energy. It's not uncommon for people who are depressed to think about death or suicide.

Long-term Opioid Use Linked to Depression

The results of a study conducted by researchers at St. Louis University and published in the *Annals of Family Medicine* have revealed that using opioids over a long period of time increases the risk of developing depression.

The researchers looked at records collected from more than 10,000 patients. The patients were treated at either the Veterans Health Administration or one of two private health-care systems. The researchers found that approximately 10 percent of them developed depression after taking opioids for more than one month.

The Substance Abuse and Mental Health Services Administration (SAMHSA) estimates that 26 percent of homeless people are drug abusers, and 38 percent abuse alcohol. Drug abuse is often a result of homelessness, rather than a cause, as people may turn to drugs or alcohol to cope with their problems. In reality, however, drug abuse decreases their ability to get a job and get off the streets.

None of the patients had depression before taking the opioids. The people in the study were taking opioids for a variety of medical conditions. They had been diagnosed with back pain, arthritis, nerve pain or muscle pain.

Even though the patients were being treated in different healthcare systems, the researchers' findings were consistent. It didn't matter where they were being treated; a significant number of patients still developed depression after being prescribed opioid pain medications for 30 days or more.

Why does opioid use lead to depression in some people? The researchers felt that the change in some patients' mental health has to do with changes opioid use causes in the user's brain. Using these types of drugs over a long time changes the brain chemistry. It influences the brain's pleasure and reward centers.

Someone who is taking an opioid pain medication that is being prescribed by their doctor should be told that they might become depressed while taking their medicine. They should see their doctor regularly for follow-up appointments. The doctor should make a point of asking the patient about their mood and if they are feeling down or "blue" during these visits. If the

Educational Video

Scan here for a video on depression, which provides information on signs, symptoms, and treatment methods:

patient does report feeling depressed, the doctor can suggest taking an antidepressant medication or seeing a therapist, or both.

Depression and Opioid Abusers

People who are using opioids which have not been prescribed for them are at risk for depression and may not be screened for this form of mental illness. This category includes people who are getting pills from family members and friends and those who are buying them on the street.

When prescription opioid users are unable to access their drug of choice, they may be forced to start using heroin. It's less expensive, and readily available. Unfortunately, from a mental health point of view, heroin raises the stakes even higher.

Heroin Users and Risk of Suicide

In 2002 the journal *Addiction* published a paper on suicide among heroin users. The authors studied available facts on suicide statistics and risk factors for those who were most likely to take their own life. They also looked at the methods heroin users used when committing suicide, compared to people who didn't use heroin.

The results of their research found that people who use heroin are at a greater risk of dying (13 times higher) than those who don't use the drug. Deaths from suicide are in the 3-35 percent range. This is 14 times higher than the average person. Rates for attempted suicide were also much higher than for non-heroin users.

In conducting their study, the authors looked at various risk factors for suicide in both heroin and non-heroin users. These included whether the person was male or female, whether they were living with a mental illness, if they had a difficult family background and if the person had few social contacts. The researchers found that heroin users were exposed to these risks, but had additional risks for suicide. They concluded that drug treatment centers need to be aware of this increased risk for their clients who are addicted to heroin.

 Text-Dependent Questions

1. How is depression different from feeling sad or "blue"?
2. Explain how heroin users are at higher risk of dying than non-users.

 Research Project

Learn about risks of suicide for young people. What are the general risks without substance abuse? Are you surprised to learn that drug abuse increases the risk of suicide? Discuss.

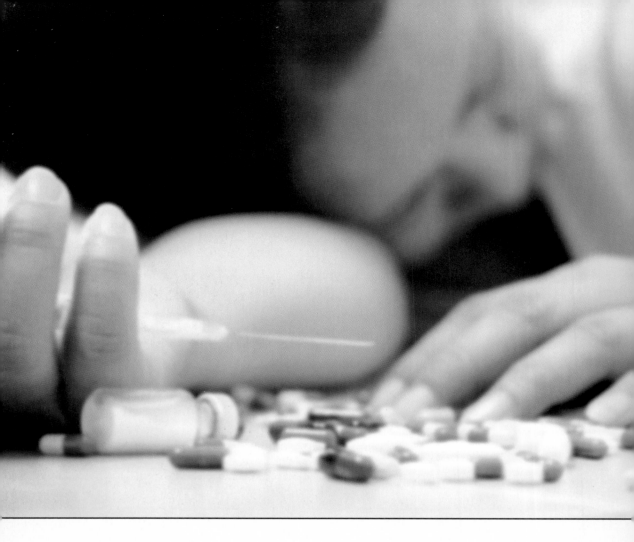

 Words to Understand in This Chapter

DUID/DUI—the crime of operating a car or other motor vehicle while impaired by drugs or alcohol. The driver must be unable to operate the vehicle safely to be found guilty.

per se—a Latin term meaning "by itself."

prohibited—illegal.

zero tolerance—a policy that imposes strict punishment for violating a rule.

Drug overdose is the leading cause of accidental death in the United States. In one recent year, the American Society of Addiction Medicine reported that there were over 52,400 lethal drug overdoses. Prescription pain pills were involved in approximately 20,100 (38 percent) of these deaths, and heroin overdoses were responsible for another 12,990 (25 percent).

4

The Ways a Drug Conviction Affect Your Life

I t's quite common for people who use drugs to feel as though they have their use under control. They feel as though they can stop using anytime they want to, and that they are able to function well, even when they are using opioids. They may even feel as though no one can tell that they are under the influence of their drug of choice, but this may not be the case. More than likely, a person's drug use is having an effect on their ability to perform everyday tasks.

Since opioid use causes a person to experience a deep sense of relaxation and drowsiness after the initial euphoria wears off, it makes sense that someone under their influence won't be as quick to respond to their environment as a person who has not used similar drugs. One situation where this can lead to potential danger is when someone drives after using opioids.

Drugged driving is as serious as drinking and driving, and has the potential to be just as deadly.

What is Drugged Driving?

Drugged driving occurs when a person operates a car, truck, bus, boat or any other motor vehicle after taking prescription or illicit drugs that make them unsafe. If the driver's drug use makes them drowsy, slows their reflexes or makes it difficult for them to focus on the road, they shouldn't be driving. They are putting themselves, their passengers and other drivers (and their passengers) at risk by being on the road.

According to a recent study by the US Department of Transportation National Highway Traffic Safety Administration (NHTSA), about 22 percent of drivers tested positive for drugs. This doesn't mean that one in five drivers are under the influence of drugs while behind the wheel, as drugs can be detected in the body days or even weeks after the period of impairment has passed. However, it does suggest that there are many drivers who have recently used drugs, and it seems likely that at least some of them are under the influence while they are driving. Recent studies by other government agencies, including the US National Survey on Drug Use and Health, have estimated that about 5 percent of licensed drivers in the United States drove under the influence of an illicit drug during the previous year.

This NHTSHA study found that the number of number of fatal traffic accidents rose by 9.3 percent in the first nine months of 2015. During that time, 26,000 people died in car accidents, compared to 23,796 for a similar period in 2014. The

Driving while under the influence of drugs—whether they are illegal drugs like heroin, or legally prescribed opioid painkillers—puts the driver, passengers, and others who share the road at risk.

NHTSA concluded that choices people were making were contributing to the increase in deaths on the road. These included drugged driving, drunk driving, speeding, drowsy driving, and failing to wear seat belts.

There are a number of consequences that can result from being stopped for drugged driving. A driver who is stopped by police can be charged with Driving Under the Influence of a Drug (*DUID*). In some places, the driver may be charged with Driving Under the Influence (*DUI*).

Since it's more difficult to detect whether someone has been using drugs than drinking alcohol, some police depart-

US Drug Schedules

The US government classifies drugs, as well as some chemicals used to manufacture drugs, in five categories, called schedules. The schedules are determined by whether a drug has an accepted use for medical purposes, as well as whether it has the potential for abuse.

Schedule I drugs have no accepted medical use and have a high potential for abuse. Heroin, marijuana, and LSD fall into this category.

Schedule II drugs do have a legitimate medical use, but they are considered dangerous because of their high potential for abuse. Opioids such as OxyContin, Dilaudid, methadone, and fentanyl are in this category, as well as other drugs like cocaine. All of these drugs can cause both physical and psychological dependence.

Schedule III drugs have a "moderate to low" potential for abuse, physical and psychological dependence. Products containing up to 90 milligrams of codeine and Suboxone, a medication used to treat opioid addiction, are both examples of drugs in this category.

Schedule IV drugs have a low potential for abuse compared to the ones listed in Schedule III. Pentazocine, an opioid pain medication that is used to treat moderate to severe pain, is an example of a drug in this category. It is usually given by injection in hospitals or clinics.

Schedule V drugs have a low potential for abuse compared to those listed in Schedule IV. Examples of drugs in this class include codeine and hydrocodone cough syrups.

ments have specially trained officers to find out whether that is the case. They are called Drug Recognition Experts (DREs). The DREs look at a person's overall behavior, as well as their eye movements and other signs to determine whether they are under the influence of drugs. A total of 44 states and the District of Columbia have DREs in place as part of their law enforcement teams.

Police can confirm whether a person has taken drugs by taking a blood or a urine sample. Most states require drivers who have been pulled over and are suspected of impairment to comply with such tests. Once the sample has been obtained, it is sent to a laboratory to be analyzed. The results of the tests can tell the police the driver has recently used opioids or other drugs.

It's possible to be charged with a crime connected with drugged driving, even if the driver was taking legally pre-scribed drugs at the time. The law only looks at whether the person's ability to operate the vehicle safely was affected.

Penalties for Drugged Driving

The penalties for drugged driving vary, depending on the state in which the offense took place. Generally speaking, there are two types of state laws that deal with drugged driving. In some states, the laws require prosecutors to prove that a drug has rendered a driver "incapable" of driving safely, or "impaired" his or her ability to operate a vehicle safely. This can be com-plicated and difficult for law-enforcement officials.

Another type of state law is known as a "*per se* statute." These laws make it a criminal offense to have a drug or intoxicating substance in one's body while operating a motor vehicle. In these states, a driver found driving with any amount of the *prohibited* substance in their system will automatically be charged with a DUID or DUI offense. These statutes are often referred to as "*zero tolerance* laws." It is much easier for a prosecutor to convict a drug-using driver under the per se statues. Today, seventeen states have per se statutes.

The substances are specified in these states' per se statutes and may be limited only to illegal drugs like heroin. In other

Conviction on drug-related charges can permanently affect a young person's ability to get into college or get hired for a good job.

Educational Video

Scan here for a news report on drugged driving and the role of DREs:

states, the substances that are covered under per se laws also include prescription pain medications like OxyContin, Dilaudid, hydromorphone, codeine and morphine.

Having a Criminal Record

A person who is convicted of possessing or selling opiates faces a number of consequences. They will have to deal with the sentence they are given by the court. Depending on the seriousness of the charge, this may include paying a fine and/or being sentenced to jail.

However, the consequences of having a criminal record do not end when the fine is paid or the jail term is served. In fact, in many ways the problems are just beginning. A criminal record related to opioid abuse will follow a person long after he or she is arrested, and will negatively affect many parts of his or her life.

For example, many employers perform background checks on applicants before they hire them for a job. Often, employers may choose not to employ a person who has a criminal record. In addition, federal and state laws bar people who have been convicted of opioid-related crimes from holding certain jobs, including the following examples:

- working in certain federal government agencies, such as the Department of Energy;
- employment at a pharmaceutical company or pharmacy, because they manufacture and distribute controlled substances;
- healthcare jobs in which the person is responsible for distributing drugs to patients;
- Working at any school or child-care facility that receives federal funding.

The law also bars people who have been convicted on drug-related charges from receiving or holding certain professional licenses. For example, a truck driver will lose his or her commercial driver's license (CDL) if they have been convicted of driving while under the influence of opioids. Someone who has been convicted of a drug-related offense is not eligible for a pilot's license, to serve on a flight crew, or to work as a merchant seaman.

Being convicted of an opioid-related crime does not just affect a person's prospects for work after college. It can also have an effect on their college studies. For example, a student convicted on drug charges is not eligible to receive any federal student loans for one year from the date of their first conviction for a first offense, or two years from the date of conviction for their second offense. After a third conviction, a person is permanently ineligible to receive any federal student loans.

Housing and a Criminal Record

The impact of having a criminal record may also affect where a person can live. A drug-related conviction makes a person ineligible for public housing; someone who is already living in public housing can have their lease cancelled. A person with a criminal record may not live in a household that is receiving food stamps.

If someone wants to rent an apartment, a criminal record involving drugs can make it more difficult for them. A prospective landlord will likely run a background check as part of the application process. It will reveal details about a person's credit history and any criminal convictions. If they have been convicted of selling or manufacturing drugs, a landlord can refuse to rent an apartment to that person—even if it has been several years since the conviction.

Travel Restrictions

Travel restrictions based on a criminal record involving controlled substances vary, depending on the country a traveler is seeking to enter. For example, the United States may restrict

 Did You Know?

A criminal record for substance abuse may bar someone from being accepted into medical school. Even if the convicted person is allowed to complete a program, they may not be eligible to become licensed to practice medicine with a conviction for a drug-related offense.

A person who is on parole or supervised release after being released from prison for a drug-related felony offense cannot be issued a passport by the US government.

entry to someone who has been convicted of possession with intent to distribute, distribution or importation of a controlled substance. The person will be banned from entering the United States for seven years, or for five years after their release from prison.

Canada has different rules about allowing travelers to enter the country. Someone who has been convicted of a crime in the United States or another country may be denied entry to Canada based on the fact that they have a prior criminal history alone. If a person is not truthful on their application or when speaking to officers at the border, they may not be allowed to enter Canada.

Each application is evaluated on a case-by-case basis. Someone who was convicted of a DUI with no jail time may be admitted to Canada for one visit. A person whose conviction is more than five years old may be able to enter Canada if the penalty for their crime in Canada is less than 10 years in prison.

Opioid abuse can affect someone's life a number of negative ways. Users don't think about the consequences at the time; however, the impact can be felt for years after the initial drug use or conviction.

 Text-Dependent Questions

1. What is drugged driving and how common is it?
2. Name some employment-related consequences of having a criminal record.
3. Can having a criminal record affect your travel plans? Explain.

 Research Project

Choose a type of career. Conduct research into the educational or training requirements someone would need to work in that field. Next, research what would happen if a person who wants to work or is working in that career had a criminal record for a controlled substance. Would they be able to pursue that career or keep working in that field?

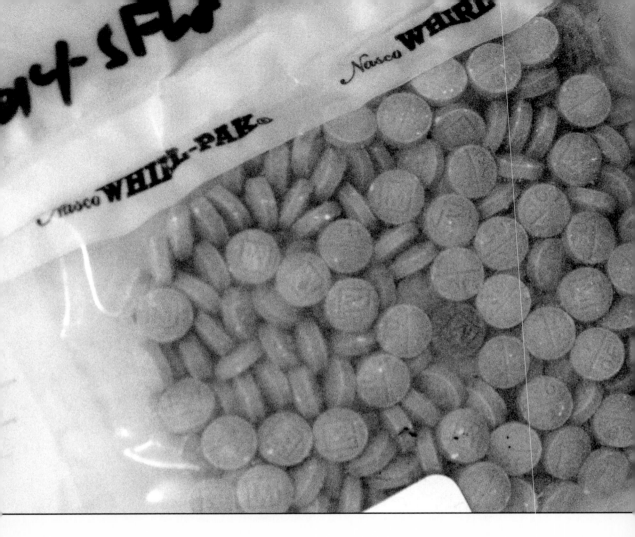

 Words to Understand in This Chapter

birth defects—abnormal health conditions that are present at birth.

fetus—an unborn human baby.

mortality—death.

stillbirth—the birth of a child who has died in the womb after at least seven months of pregnancy.

5

A bag of Fentanyl pills seized in a DEA raid. Because Fentanyl causes effects similar to heroin, the two drugs are sometimes mixed when sold illegally in order to increase the potency of low-grade heroin. However, including too much Fentanyl in the mix can lead to a deadly overdose, as the drug is much stronger than heroin.

The Effects of Opioids on Families

The dangers of drug abuse from opioids extend to future generations too. Women who are, or who may become pregnant need to be aware if they use these types of drugs, they may be causing harm to an unborn child. When parents are drug users or abusers, they may be putting their own lives at risk, which has serious consequences for their children. In either case, drug abuse has the potential to alter the course of a young person's life.

Opioid Abuse and Pregnancy

In a perfect world, pregnant women would avoid any substances that could possibly harm a growing *fetus*. In reality, a woman who is using opioids and was not planning to have a baby can become pregnant. Such a person may be unwilling to tell her doctor she is using opioids, especially if she is getting them on the street.

This presents a problem, since opioid use during pregnancy can lead to many problems for the unborn baby. Heroin use can cause premature birth, as well as *stillbirth*. It can also lead to *birth defects* and NAS (Neonatal Abstinence Syndrome).

Opioid Treatment for Pregnant Women

Some pregnant women who are addicted to opioids hesitate to ask about treatment during pregnancy because they are concerned that they will be treated as criminals. They have good reasons to be concerned. In the United States, the state of Tennessee has passed a law making substance abuse during pregnancy a crime. In twenty-four other states, as well as in the District of Columbia, using drugs while pregnant is considered to be child abuse. In three of these states—Minnesota, South Dakota, and Wisconsin—a pregnant woman who uses drugs can be forced to enter an inpatient treatment program.

Some people feel that a pregnant woman should be encouraged to get treatment for her opioid use and that this matter

 ## Educational Video

Scan here to see a heartbreaking video on babies who are born with NAS due to opioid-addicted parents:

Neonatal Abstinence Syndrome

Neonatal Abstinence Syndrome (NAS) occurs when a baby is exposed to drugs before being born. When a pregnant woman uses opioids, her unborn baby also experiences their effects. After the baby is born, the infant no longer has a source for the opioid drugs and can experience withdrawal symptoms in the same way that a junkie trying to quit heroin would.

Babies born with NAS need to have specialized treatment in hospital, because severe cases can be fatal. Infants with this syndrome are more likely to have a low birthweight (under five pounds, eight ounces), as well as difficulties with basic functions like eating and breathing. As a result, these babies are more likely to have to stay in the hospital longer than babies who do not have NAS.

Neonatal Abstinence Syndrome can be diagnosed by observing symptoms (excessive fussiness and crying, difficulty feeding, shaking, difficulty sleeping, fever, and sweating) and testing a urine sample. If a baby has NAS, he or she can be given drugs, such as methadone, to treat the symptoms of withdrawal. The methadone doses are decreased over time as opioid withdrawal become controlled.

should be treated as a public health matter instead of a criminal one. The best choice that a pregnant woman can make for herself and her child is to be honest with her doctor about what she is taking and seek appropriate treatment.

For pregnant women, appropriate treatment looks different from how opioid abuse is normally dealt with. Going off opioids abruptly is not recommended, since it could cause the woman to go into labor too early or cause harm to the developing fetus. The recommended treatment for pregnant women with opioid abuse or addiction issues is treatment with

The twenty-four states that consider drug use while pregnant to be child abuse include: Alabama, Arizona, Arkansas, Colorado, Florida, Illinois, Indiana, Iowa, Louisiana, Maryland, Minnesota, Missouri, Nevada, North Dakota, Ohio, Oklahoma, Rhode Island, South Carolina, South Dakota, Texas, Utah, Virginia, Washington, and Wisconsin. The District of Columbia also considers drug use while pregnant to be child abuse.

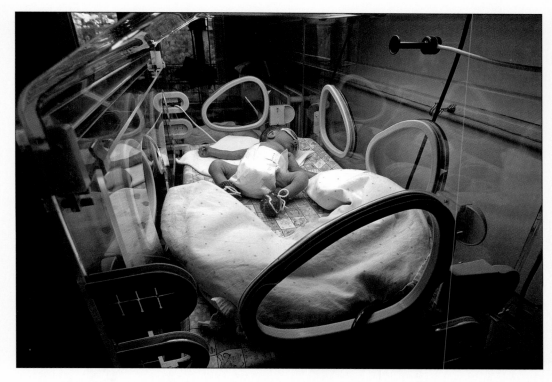

Since 1999, the number of babies born with NAS in the United States has tripled. The rate was 1.5 per 1,000 hospital births in 1999; today it is 6 per 1,000 births.

methadone to deal with the cravings for opioids. Ideally, the woman would be able to get counseling to help her develop strategies to avoid using opioids again and to deal with underlying reasons for her substance abuse issue.

Early Death Due to Opioid Overdose

As doctors continue to prescribe opioid pain medications, the risk of overdose increases. According to the Centers for Disease Control and Prevention (CDC), the number of deaths caused by opioid overdoses have quadrupled since the year 1999.

All-cause mortality, age 45-54, for US white non-Hispanics (USW), US Hispanics, and six comparison countries: France (FRA), Germany (GER), the United Kingdom (UK), Canada (CAN), Australia (AUS), and Sweden (SWE).

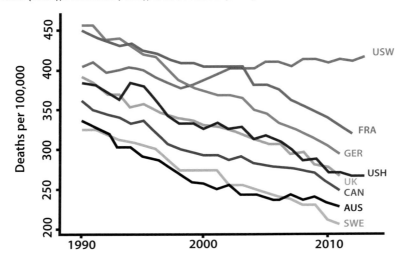

Mortality by cause, US white non-Hispanics age 45-54.

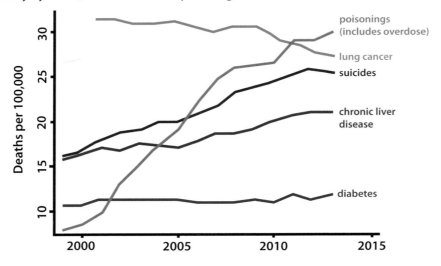

Source: Anne Case and Angus Deaton, "Rising morbidity and mortality in midlife among white non-Hispanic Americans in the 21st century," *PNAS* 112, no. 49 (December 8, 2015), pp. 15078–15083. http://www.pnas.org/content/112/49/15078.full.pdf

According to the most recent data, in the period from 1999 to 2015, more than 183,000 people have lost their lives to prescription drug overdoses. In 2015 alone, more than 15,000 people died in this manner.

Anne Case and Angus Deaton, of the Woodrow Wilson Public and International Affairs and Department of Economics, Princeton University, published a paper where they shared the results of their research on *mortality* rates of white men and women since the 1990s. The two researchers were looking at the fact that rates jumped at this point in time compared to other countries. They found that the increase was not due to age-related factors, such as heart disease, stroke or diabetes. Instead, it was linked to overdoses of prescription painkillers and alcohol. The higher death rates were also due to suicide.

All of the numbers in these statistics about deaths due to drug overdoses represent real people. They may have had parents, or been parents themselves. If their death was accidental, they weren't planning to end their life on the day they died.

 Did You Know?

Nearly 50 percent of teens in the United States believe that prescription drugs are much safer than illicit street drugs. In addition, one out of eight high school seniors report using prescription opioids for non-medical purposes. And seven out of 10 non-medical users reported mixing prescription drugs with alcohol and/or at least one other drug in the past year—which puts them at a substantial risk for overdose.

When one or both parents die as the result of a drug overdose, it creates a hole in a family that can't be filled. If the children in the family are not yet adults, they will either be sent to live with a family member, or placed in the foster care system.

Drug overdose statistics show that there is a real issue with middle-aged people abusing opioids in the United States. This age group may well have children who could be affected by their drug use. We run the risk of more children growing up in situations where they are not being raised by their parents, and

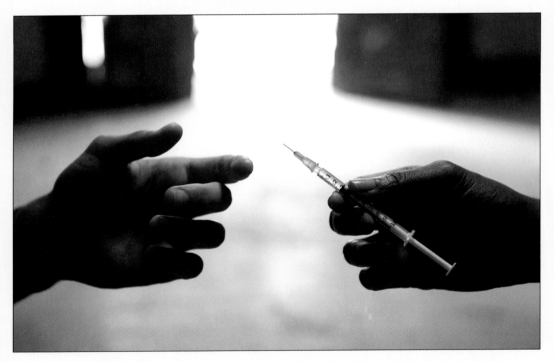

Drug use increases a person's risk for contracting a viral infection. Diseases can be spread when people inject drugs and share dirty needles or other paraphernalia. These practices put users at a higher risk of infection with HIV, the virus that causes AIDS. Hepatitis, a disease that can cause liver damage, is another danger. In addition, when drug use impairs a person's judgment that person may make unwise choices about intimate contact, resulting in the spread of sexually transmitted diseases (STDs).

these children may carry that burden into adulthood. Some of them may even be at higher risk for drug abuse and addiction themselves.

This is just one of many ways that drug addiction and abuse has a terrible effect on future generations. However, no one is doomed to become an addict simply because a parent had a problem with opioids. The dangers of drug abuse are very real, but with education that helps young people to make good choices, it is possible to minimize those dangers.

 Text-Dependent Questions

1. Name five states where women may be charged with child abuse for using drugs while pregnant. Does this law apply where you live?
2. It's dangerous for a pregnant woman to go off opioids all at once. Why?

 Research Project

Divide your class in half. One group is assigned to write a brief paper giving reasons why pregnant women should be arrested and jailed for using opioids if it means protecting their unborn children. The other group is assigned to write a paper giving reasons why pregnant women should be encouraged to seek treatment, but their drug use not be reported to authorities. After the papers are written, one person from each group shares their work with the other. Can you make the other person understand your point of view on this complicated issue?

Series Glossary

analgesic—any member of a class of drugs used to achieve analgesia, or relief from pain.

central nervous system—the part of the human nervous system that consists of the brain and spinal cord. These are greatly affected by opiates and opioids.

dependence—a situation that occurs when opiates or opioids are used so much that the user's body adapts to the drug and only functions normally when the drug is present. When the user attempts to stop using the drug, a physiologic reaction known as withdrawal syndrome occurs.

epidemic—a widespread occurrence of a disease or illness in a community at a particular time.

opiates—a drug that is derived directly from the poppy plant, such as opium, heroin, morphine, and codeine.

opioids—synthetic drugs that affect the body in a similar way as opiate drugs. The opioids include Oxycotin, hydrocodone, fentanyl, and methadone.

withdrawal—a syndrome of often painful physical and psychological symptoms that occurs when someone stops using an addictive drug, such as an opiate or opioid. Often, the drug user will begin taking the drug again to avoid withdrawal.

Further Reading

Darnall, Beth, Ph.D. *Less Pain, Fewer Pills*. Boulder: Bull Publishing Company, 2014.

Gammill, Joani. *Painkillers, Heroin, and the Road to Sanity*. Center City, MN: Hazelden, 2014.

Glass, George, M.D. *Narcotics: Dangerous Painkillers*. New York: Rosen Publishing Group, 2001.

Knight, A.J. *Opiate Withdrawal: How to Kick Opiates, Cure Your Addiction And Make it Through the Detox Withdrawals*. CreateSpace, 2015.

Quinones, Sam. *Dreamland: The True Tale of America's Opiate Epidemic*. New York: Bloomsbury Press, 2015.

Sheff, David. *Clean: Overcoming Addiction and Ending America's Greatest Tragedy*. New York: Houghton Mifflin Harcourt, 2013.

Vest, David. *Making Millions, Making Monsters: My Experience Working in the Field of Opiate Replacement Therapy*. Amazon, 2014.

Wiles, Justin. *Through an Addict's Eyes: Day in the Life of an Addict*. Amazon, 2017.

Internet Resources

www.cdc.gov/drugoverdose/prescribing/patients.html

The CDC maintains a webpage with helpful information for patients who are prescribed opioids to learn about the drugs and dangers associated with them.

www.ccsa.ca

This website delivers a wide range of publications on substance abuse in Canada. Subjects relate to prescription drugs and alcohol, drug treatment, impaired driving, abuse prevention, and other drug-related topics.

www.samhsa.gov

A vast amount of research related to opioids and other substances can be performed on the Substance Abuse and Mental Health Services Administration website. The website also provides resources on national strategies and initiatives, state and local initiatives, and training and education.

www.dea.gov/druginfo/factsheets.shtml

The Drug Enforcement Administration (DEA) maintains fact sheets on numerous narcotics, hallucinogens, stimulants, depressants, and other drugs of concern.

www.drugfreeworld.org/real-life-stories/heroin.html

The Foundation for a Drug-Free World provides a video and real life quotes from heroin addicts.

https://easyread.drugabuse.gov/

The National Institute on Drug Abuse maintains a webpage called Easy-to-Read Drug Facts that contains short videos, drug profiles, and personal stories of teens in recovery.

www.nar-anon.org/

Nar-Anon is a 12-step program for the families and friends of addicts with meetings all over the world.

www.painmed.org/

The American Academy of Pain Medicine's website provides current and relevant information on pain medicine, including clinical reference resources and the latest news on pain research.

www.cihi.ca/en

The Canadian Institute for Health Information website offers a National Prescription Drug Utilization Information System (NPDUIS) Database that stores pan-Canadian information on public drug programs.

Index

addiction, drug. *See* drug addiction

age-related diseases, 24–27

alcohol, 8, 28, 29, 30, *32*, 55
    combination of, with opioids, 26, 27
    and driving, 36, 39
    See also drug addiction

Alia-Klein, Nelly, 26

atarax, 16

birth defects, 48, 50
    See also pregnancy

"black tar" heroin, *15*, 18
    See also heroin

brain chemistry, 7–13, 20–22, 24, 26, 33
    See also drug addiction

buprenorphine, 16

Canada, 46–47

Case, Anne, 55

child abuse laws, 50, 52

chronic pain, 9, 15–16, *17*, 20, *23*, 33
    See also prescription pain medications

codeine, *7*, 9, 16, 17, 18, 40, 43

convictions, drug, *42*, 43–44
    and drugged driving, 36, 37–39, 41–43, 44
    and housing, 45
    and per se laws, 36, 41–43
    and travel restrictions, 45–47
    See also drug addiction

deaths, overdose, 15, 20, 21, *37*, 53, 55–57

Deaton, Angus, 55

demerol, 16

depression, 30–34
    See also mental health issues

Dilaudid, 9, 16, 40, 43

dopamine, 8, 11, 20–21

driving, drugged, 36, 37–39, 41–43, 44

drug addiction
    and age-related diseases, 24–27
    and brain chemistry, 7–13, 20–22, 24, 26, 33
    definition of, 7–8
    development of, 8–9, 21
    and disease risks, *56*
    and drug convictions, 36, 41–44, *42*, 45–47
    and drugged driving, 36, 37–39, 41–43, 44
    and a dual diagnosis, 28, 29–30
    and family life, 49–53, 55–57
    and mental health issues, 28, 29–35
    number of people with, *12*, 21, *32*
    and overdose deaths, 15, 20, 21, *37*, 53, 55–57
    and self-medication, 28, 30
    treatments for, 18–19, 40, 52–53
    and withdrawal, 14, 18, 22–23, 51
    See also alcohol; opioids

drug dependence, 14, 22–23

Drug Recognition Experts (DREs), 41

drug schedules, 40

drugged driving, 36, 37–39, 41–43, 44
    See also convictions, drug

dual diagnosis, 28, 29–30

DUID/DUI charges, 36, 39, 41–42
    See also drugged driving

Numbers in ***bold italic*** refer to captions.

endorphins (neurotransmitters), *10*, 12
enkephaline (neurotransmitter), *10*

family life, 49–53
   and early deaths, 55–57
fentanyl, *7*, 9, 15, 16, 20, 40, *49*

gamma-aminobutyric acid (GABA), 11

heroin, *7*, 9, *10*, 16, 17, 40
   and age-related diseases, 26, 27
   "black tar," *15*, 18
   and number of users, *12*, 21
   and overdose deaths, 15, 20, *37*, *49*
   and pregnancy, 50, 51
   and suicide, 34–35
   types of, *15*, 18
   See also opioids
Hippocrates, 9
homelessness, *32*
housing, 45
hydrocodine, 17
hydrocodone, *7*, *29*, 40
hydromorphone, 17, 20, 43

Juurlink, David, 15

lortab, 16

mental health issues, 28, 29–30
   and depression, 30–34
   and suicide, *31*, 34–35
methadone, 9, 16, 40
   and treatment of drug addiction,
     18–19, 51, 53
morphine, *7*, 9, 11, 16, 17–18, 43
mortality rates, 48, 55–56
mu-opioid receptors (MORs), 20–21
   See also brain chemistry

naloxone, 11–12, 16
naltrexone, 16
Neonatal Abstinence Syndrome (NAS),
   50, 51, *53*
   See also pregnancy
nephropathy, 14, 27
neurotransmitters, 6, 9–11, 12, 20–21
   See also brain chemistry
norco, 16

opiates, 8, 9, 11–12, 16

opioids
   and brain chemistry, *10*, 12, 20–22,
     33
   definition of, 9, 16
   and drug schedules, 40
   and drug tolerance, 21–22
   and drugged driving, 36, 37–39,
     41–43, 44
   and mental health issues, 30–35
   and mu-opioid receptors (MORs),
     20–21
   and overdose deaths, 15, 20, 21, *37*,
     53, 55–57
   and permanent body changes,
     24–27, 33
   and pregnancy, 49–53
   as prescription pain medications, *7*,
     15–16, *17*, 20, 21, *23*, 33–34, *37*,
     41, 43, 55
   types of, *7*, 16, 17–20, *29*
   See also drug addiction
opium, 17, 22
orpivaine, 16
overdose deaths, 15, 20, 21, *37*, 53,
   55–57
   See also drug addiction
oxycodone, *7*, 9, 16–17, 19–20
OxyContin, 16, 19–20, 40, 43
oxymorphone, 16

pain. *See* chronic pain
palliative care, 14, 15
pentazocine, 40
per se laws, 36, 41–43
   See also convictions, drug
Pert, Candace, 11–12
poppy, opium, 9, 13, 16, 17
   See also opioids
pregnancy, 49–53
prescription pain medications, *7*,
   15–16, *17*, 20, 21
   and depression, 33–34
   and drugged driving, 41, 43
   and overdose deaths, *37*, 55
   and teens, 55
   and women, *23*
   See also opioids

research projects, 13, 27, 35, 47, 57
reuptake, 11
   See also brain chemistry

schedules, drug, 40
self-medication, 28, 30
    See also drug addiction
semisynthetic opioids, 14, 16–17, *29*
    See also opioids
serotonin, 11
Snyder, Solomon, 11–12
stillbirth, 48, 50
    See also pregnancy
Suboxone, 40
substance P, 11
suicide, *31*, 34–35, 55
    See also mental health issues
synthetic opioids, 16, 19, *29*
    See also opioids

teens, *12*, 55
thebaine, 16, 17
traffic accidents, 38–39
    See also drugged driving
travel restrictions, 45–47

vascular dementia, 14, 26
Vicodin, 9

withdrawal, 14, 19, 22–23, 51
    See also drug addiction

zero tolerance laws, 36, 42

About the Author

Jodee Redmond has been working as a freelance writer since 2000. Jodee has co-hosted an Internet radio program, written a newspaper column, and been a guest lecturer at the University of Western Ontario. Jodee is the author of *The Secret Sauce to Freelance Writing on the Side"* (2017). She lives in London, Ontario, with her husband, two daughters, and a rescue cat named Crimson.